TEMPLE RUN™
TAKE CONTROL OF THIS STORY
IF YOU DARE
GET READY TO
RUN FOR YOUR LIFE!

EGMONT
USA
New York

With special thanks to Adrian Bott

EGMONT
We bring stories to life

First published in the United Kingdom by Egmont UK Limited, 2014
First published in the United States of America by Egmont USA, 2014
443 Park Avenue South, Suite 806
New York, NY 10016
Cover illustration by Jacopo Camagni
Interior illustrations by Artful Doodlers

1 3 5 7 9 8 6 4 2
www.ImangiStudios.com
www.egmontusa.com
ISBN 978-1-60684-571-4
eBook ISBN 978-1-60684-574-5

Printed in the United States of America

1

"We're clear for takeoff!"

Guy Dangerous leans back from the pilot's chair to give you a grin and a thumbs-up.

This is going to be the best birthday party ever. You can't believe your luck, winning a whole weekend on your very own private beach, complete with cookout, scavenger hunt, Jet-Skiing . . . you can't wait to get underway. The prize is just for you and five of your closest, hand-picked friends, all expenses paid.

Usually, having a birthday during a school break means having to do stuff with the whole family, but this time there are strictly no parents. This time, it's an *adventure*.

You sit and look through your winner's letter and the shiny brochures, thinking of the awesome time that awaits at the other end of this plane ride.

"Hang on!" calls Scarlett Fox from the seat next to yours. "I think our VIP's forgotten something."

2

What can she—oh, right. In all the excitement, you've forgotten to fasten your seat belt. It clicks as you slot it into position.

Scarlett nods and makes a final check on her checklist. "Five by five. We're good to go."

Guy slips on some dark glasses. He flicks a switch and "La Macarena" blasts into the cabin. "Thanks for flying Dangerous Airlines. We do our best *not* to live up to our name, but if you need to throw up, please do it into your own lap and not someone else's . . ."

"Guy, be a darling and shut it, would you?" Scarlett says sweetly.

"Roger that."

3

The engines roar, the plane picks up speed, and your stomach suddenly lurches as the wheels leave the ground.

Scarlett pulls a laptop from her bag—how many gadgets can one woman have, you wonder—and flips it open. "Just emailing your parents to say we're in the air," she tells you. "Aha. Looks like your guests are on their way, too. So far, so good!"

"Don't jinx it," Guy growls.

Scarlett snaps her laptop shut. "There. All done. That's the last the outside world will hear from us for a while."

Scarlett Fox has to be the most organized person you've ever met. The competition runners knew what they were doing when they picked the smart, red-haired British woman to be your party planner. She's thought of everything in advance.

As for Guy Dangerous, your unshaven pilot, he looks like he just rolled out of bed and into his combat boots. But the wisecracking American knows the wilderness, and that's just what you need in a tour guide. You've seen a few episodes of his reality TV show, *Whatever It Takes*, featuring Guy showing celebrities how to survive in the wild. Everyone's seen the one where he talks the runway model into eating the five-inch caterpillar. *Yuck*.

You just have to hope he doesn't take any crazy risks, like the ones that got him fired from the TV show . . . but you don't imagine he can get into too much trouble on a tropical beach. Maybe he'll try to find an octopus to wrestle or something.

The hours in the air pass easily. You play games on your brand-new tablet, another part of your competition prize. Guy hums, drinks coffee, and jokes with you. Scarlett checks and re-checks the contents of her bag—"a first-aid kit, mosquito repellent, flares"—and charts your position on a GPS hooked up to her laptop. Right now, the plane's flying over a screenful of bright green.

You look out the window. The jungle below covers the landscape like thick moss. Towering trees loom up out of it. You're flying so low, it's like you could reach out and touch the leaves.

"Hey, Scarlett! Why'd you bring all that junk, anyway?" Guy shouts over the noise of the engines. "There'll be supplies at Palomar Beach."

Scarlett wrinkles her nose. "It's best to be prepared for anything. You never know what might happen."

Guy snorts. "Give me a good sharp machete over your bag of tricks any day of the week."

Just then, you hear something odd that makes you sit up in your seat. Did one of the engines just . . . well . . . *sputter*?

Maybe you're hearing things. Guy and Scarlett don't seem to have noticed it . . . or if they did, they're ignoring it.

"Hey, check out the view! See the mountains?" Guy points out two peaks above the jungle.

"The Horns of the Sleeping God. That's what the folklore calls them," says Scarlett. "We're halfway to Palomar Beach, folks!"

"Woo-hoo!" you cheer, pumping a fist in the air . . .

. . . and that's when the engines start to shudder.

6

Nobody speaks for a few horrible seconds. Then you hear the voice of Guy Dangerous: "Awww, *no*, you've got to be kidding me!"

"What's going on?" you yell.

"We're losing altitude!" He slaps the dashboard.

Scarlett glances your way. "I'm sure it's nothing to worry about," she says coolly. "Guy's a professional. He can handle a little hiccup like this. Right, Guy?"

Guy's only answer is a grunt. Meanwhile, the engines gasp like they're running out of breath.

"We've got a problem," Guy eventually says. "A *big* problem. Fuel line must have come loose or something, because . . . the tanks are empty. We're running on fumes."

"Can we make it to an airport?" you ask.

"Kid, we won't even make it over this jungle."

He's not joking. "What?" you yell.

"I know! This is crazy. There was plenty of fuel when we took off."

"Did you check?" Scarlett snaps.

"Yes! I mean, I'm pretty sure."

"Now you're only 'pretty sure'! Do I have to remind you of everything?"

Guy struggles with the controls. He does his best to level the plane, but you know deep down that you're not going to reach Palomar Beach for a long time. Maybe not ever. Even the best pilot in the world can't make a plane fly without fuel.

That jungle outside the window looks a lot closer now. The engines rattle and gargle like they're choking to death. You know where the emergency parachutes are, because of Scarlett's pre-flight briefing, but you never thought you might actually need to use them.

"We're going down," Guy says, sounding grim. "Hold on tight!"

You crane your head around so you can see into the cockpit. The fuel needle is in the red, and a warning light's flashing. How could Guy have missed that? And how come checking the fuel tank wasn't on one of Scarlett's checklists?

Outside, the jungle rushes past, so close you can

see the leaves on the trees. It's enough to freeze you with fear. Those tree trunks will rip off the bottom of this plane if you drop any lower.

"Going to set her down by the foot of the mountains," grunts Guy. "I'm not going to lie . . . this'll be a bumpy landing!"

You quickly get into the crash-landing position. Head down, hug your knees, and hope. Beside you, Scarlett does the same. She's even got an inflatable impact cushion ready. That woman is prepared for anything.

"Sorry, kid," says Guy. He sounds like he really means it.

Scarlett hollers, "Don't bother with apologies, you oaf! Just get us through this alive!"

There's a deafening crash. You feel like all your bones have been knocked out of your body. The plane hits the ground, bumps up, hits again. There's a screech of torn metal as one of the wings is ripped away from the fuselage. You hear breaking glass and smell gasoline. Then everything goes dark . . .

★

"Hey! You're awake!"

You sit up groggily. You're in a rocky clearing, surrounded by debris. Your plane—what's left of it—lies in a mangled wreck just outside the tree line. Your arms and legs ache, but you know you're lucky to be alive at all.

Guy passes you a cup of water. You notice the bandage around his head. "Oh, yeah," he says. "Took a knock on the dashboard as we went down. Good thing I have a hard head!"

"Scarlett?" you ask. "Did she . . . ?"

"She's fine!" Guy says quickly. "Walked away without a scratch. She's tougher than she looks, you know."

At that moment, you hear Scarlett yelp. She comes tumbling out of the remains of the cockpit, holding a black box you recognize as the radio.

"Gotcha!" she says, standing up and dusting herself off. "It didn't want to come out, but I persuaded it. OK, let's see if this works."

10

You're not sure if the radio is broken or what, but Scarlett can't get anything other than a hissing whine out of it. As she fusses and sighs, you ask Guy what happened to her GPS and laptop.

Guy just jerks a thumb at the wrecked plane. "Don't ask. She's in a bad enough mood already. Want to help me drag out the emergency supplies?"

Soon, you're all sitting together among what's left of the supplies.

Scarlett's managed to rescue some of her gizmos. She's even begun a new checklist. "OK. We have enough water for three, maybe four days. The food will last us a day at most. We're miles away from civilization, we're not on any known flight paths, there's thick jungle in every direction, and the sun's going down in three hours. Any questions?"

You've got one. "What should we do about it?"

"That's what I like to see!" Guy grins. "A can-do attitude!"

"I say we split up and head out in different directions," says Scarlett.

11

Guy agrees. "Whoever reaches civilization first can send help back for the others."

You look over your shoulder at the looming jungle. Thick vines hang down like webs. There's no telling what might be lurking between those huge tree trunks. You think over Scarlett's words and wonder why you aren't on any known flight paths. Do regular airline flights avoid this jungle for some reason? Was Guy taking risks again, flying the plane somewhere he shouldn't have?

"Actually . . . maybe you shouldn't head off on your own," Scarlett tells you. "Buddy up with me. Safer that way."

"Or with *me*," Guy says, hands on his hips.

What do you want to do? It's up to you! Guy Dangerous loves to take risks. But he's also a well-known survival expert. On the other hand, Scarlett Fox is super organized and has a bag full of useful high-tech gadgets.

Then again, the three of you could cover more ground if you went off alone. Maybe you're tough enough to handle the jungle without anyone's help. They may be adults, but Guy and Scarlett haven't exactly kept you out of danger so far, have they?

To go with Guy, turn to page 61.

To go with Scarlett, turn to page 51.

Or, if you want to head off on your own, turn to page 81.

"You go first," you tell Guy. "I'll wait here."

Guy sets off across the bridge, taking it at a run. Halfway across, his foot goes straight through one of the planks. He catches himself in time—"Watch your step!" he says—and keeps running. You've got a bad feeling about this.

A grunting, snorting noise comes from the jungle. You freeze.

There's some kind of animal out there. You glimpse its hulking form moving between the trees. What is that thing? It's too big to be a human. You smell something bad, like rotting food.

"Hey!" Guy yells from his side of the bridge. "It's safe. Come on over!"

The thing in the jungle makes the grunting noise again. It's definitely getting closer. Time to leave. You run out onto the bridge.

Luckily, it holds your weight. Some of the boards creak and one of the ropes snaps suddenly, but you make it to the other side with nothing worse than a few rattled nerves.

"There's some sort of creature in the jungle," you tell Guy.

"Did you get a look at it?"

"Not much of one. It's big, though."

Guy thinks for a moment. Before you can stop him, he's pulled his machete out and hacked through the ropes holding the bridge up. It falls and smashes against the cliff on the other side.

You gawk at him. "What did you do *that* for?"

"If there's something weird out there, we don't want it following us," Guy says.

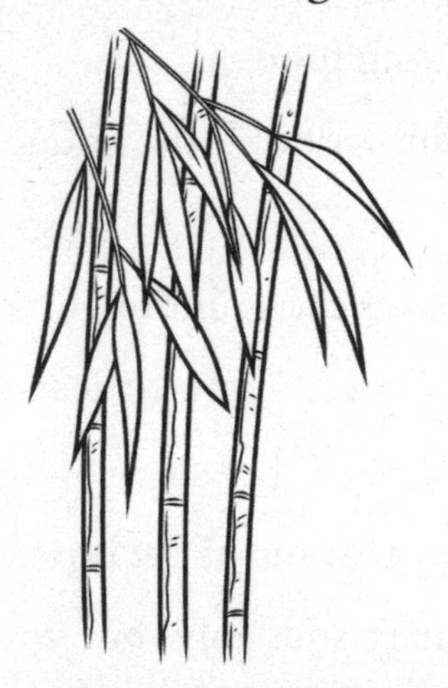

You glance over your shoulder. He's got a point. Time to press on. You head into the jungle, looking for any sign of civilization.

Run on to page 25.

Whump! You fall free from the zip-line and land, rolling over and over, on the far side. Scarlett follows you across the same way. "See?" she gasps. "Nothing to it."

You look up ahead, to see where the mysterious stone path leads. It's overgrown with scrub and jungle ferns, but you can still see it turns into a set of steps that lead up the side of some kind of structure.

"I think it's a building," you tell Scarlett.

"The temple?" Scarlett says, her eyes wild with excitement. She starts to run and almost falls over a sprawling skeleton, half-hidden by the vegetation.

You run along after her. The skeleton, you're glad to see, is only that of some animal, maybe a goat or a sheep. Funny how Scarlett didn't even give it a second glance.

You pound up the stone steps and realize you're climbing the side of a low, flat tower as broad across as a football field. It must have been part of a city's defenses once.

What you see next stops you dead in your tracks.

16

Scarlett stares, too. There's a helicopter parked on the flat stone surface. It's gleaming and black, and looks very expensive. Along the tail run the words:

ZACK WONDER
ENTERPRISES INTERNATIONAL

"Zack Wonder?" you say. "Like, the super-famous football player?"

"Who else could afford this?" Scarlett glances around desperately. "It's his personal chopper. So he must be here somewhere! But *why* is anyone's guess."

There doesn't seem to be anyone around, though. No pilot, no owner . . . nothing.

"We could fly it out of here," you suggest. "I mean, we *are* stranded."

"Let me see . . ." Scarlett fiddles with the electronic key, prodding and poking with some technical tools from her bag. Eventually, she manages to start the engine. For the first time since you met her, she doesn't seem to know what she's doing.

"Do you mind if I have a go?" you ask politely.

Scarlett raises an eyebrow. "You can fly a chopper?" She looks very reluctant about the idea.

"How hard can it be?" You've practiced enough times in video games, after all. All this electronic wizardry in the cockpit should keep you safe. Modern helicopters pretty much fly themselves, don't they?

If you'd prefer Scarlett to fly the helicopter, go to page 28.

To insist on flying it yourself, go to page 65.

If you'd rather explore the wider area in the hope of finding the helicopter's owner, go to page 71.

18

"Whoa," says Guy, impressed. "Check *that* out! Nice view."

The path has led you to the edge of a ravine, where the jungle falls away in steep cliffs on either side. Down at the bottom, a rushing river foams over sharp-looking rocks. There's a rope bridge leading across to the other side. A small, dead-looking tree hangs over the cliff edge on that end, dangling its branches into the ravine.

You're not sure, but you think you can see the shapes of tents or huts through the trees on the far

side. You wish you had a pair of binoculars. Scarlett probably has some in her bag of tricks, wherever she is now.

You take a better look at that rope bridge. *Gulp*. A narrow, swaying bridge across a ravine is scary enough, but the more you look at it, the more you wonder just how long it's been there. It's not in good shape. Some of the planks are missing and the old ropes look about as sturdy as dental floss.

Before you can stop him, Guy Dangerous has already run to the bridge and is starting to cross it!

"Guy!" you shout. "Wait up!"

He holds out his hands. "What's the problem?"

The bridge creaks ominously under his weight . . .

You could cross the bridge with Guy. Safety in numbers and all that . . . **Go to page 20.**

Or you could wait for Guy to cross first, then cross the bridge yourself. **Turn to page 13.**

Or if you want to run back into the jungle, **turn to page 40.**

"We should cross together for safety," you suggest.

With Guy in front and you right behind, you step out onto the bridge. You grip the hand ropes to steady yourself. One step at a time, you move away from the edge and across the terrifying drop. Every gust of wind makes the whole bridge sway—and your stomach lurch.

"Easy," Guy says. "Relax, you're doing fine!"

These ancient, weathered planks don't look safe at all. You put your weight on one and it snaps right in two, like a dry twig. You manage to steady yourself, but the sight of the wooden pieces tumbling into the river far, far below makes you break into a cold sweat.

"I'm OK!" you tell Guy, who is looking at you, worried.

The next moment, a slow creaking noise catches your attention. A rope snaps, then another. The bridge sags alarmingly.

It's giving way! *This old bridge isn't strong enough*

to take two people at once, you think, panicked.

"Run!" yells Guy.

You can feel the bridge breaking free of its moorings as you desperately sprint for the far end. The planks beneath your feet lurch like a ship in a storm, threatening to pitch you into empty space.

Guy runs ahead, jumps off the collapsing bridge, and grabs hold of one of the branches hanging from the dead-looking tree. He turns and holds his hand out to you. "Trust me, I won't let you fall!" he yells.

The bridge starts to buckle as its last few moorings break. You have only seconds to decide what to do.

To jump off the bridge and try to grab Guy's outstretched hand, go to page 23.

Or you could grab the hand rope, hold on tight, and hope for the best. Turn to page 32.

You grab Guy's hand in yours. For a terrifying second, you dangle over a treacherous drop, watching the remains of the bridge tumble down and smash into the foam. The tree branch groans under your weight. You hear rocks rattle as the tree roots start to pull free.

"Hurry, kid!" says Guy. "You're going to have to climb up me and onto the tree. It won't be dignified, but it's our only chance."

He's right, you realize. There's no other choice. You pull yourself up Guy, using his body like a rope ladder. Soon you're hanging onto the tree with your feet on Guy's shoulders. Guy takes it well, and doesn't even complain when you accidentally tread on his face.

"Sorry!" you gasp.

"Eh, I've had worse." Then, to your surprise, he giggles. "Hurry up! There's a centipede or something crawling up my arm. It's tickling! I can't hold on . . ."

You put on a burst of speed. Grab an upper branch, heave, swing—and you're sprawling on firm ground at the cliff top, safe and sound. No time to celebrate, though. You straddle the tree trunk and reach down to help Guy up.

Guy pulls his shirt open. You stare. A spider the size of a saucer is climbing across Guy's chest.

Guy just shrugs, cups it in his hands, and lets it go on the ground. "Cute little fellow."

You gasp. "Isn't that species deadly?"

"No," Guy says. "They're good eating, though. Especially the legs. Crunchy."

You wonder if Guy's enjoying this situation more than he's letting on. Together, you head away from the ruined bridge and into the jungle, toward the shapes that look like tents or huts.

Run on to page 25.

You and Guy run down the jungle path to a clearing. There are five or six crude huts here, each one hung with colorful tie-dyed cloth. So there are people living here after all! You can smell something cooking nearby, spicy and rich. There are no vehicles around, but you can see tire marks in the middle of the clearing.

"Hey!" yells Guy. "Anyone home?" You roll your eyes. So much for the advantage of surprise.

A tie-dyed door hanging opens, and an old man with a round belly strolls out. With his gray beard and glasses he looks kind of like Santa, except for the headband and the beach shorts he's got on.

"Duuuude," he says in a slow drawl. "No need to, like, shout. You're disturbing the peace of the forest, you know?"

"Our plane crashed," you explain. "We're trying to get back to civilization."

The old guy chuckles. "Ain't that funny. Me and the other guys, we moved out here twenty years ago to get *away* from civilization."

He seems friendly, so you get to talking. Franklin (that's his name) doesn't have a phone, a radio, or any other way to contact the outside world. These people really aren't big on technology. About the only modern thing they own is a truck, which makes the hundred-mile trip to the nearest town once a week for supplies. That's where all the other dudes have gone.

"So can we get a lift out of here in your truck?" you ask him.

"Sure, dude. It'll be back in, oh, three days."

Three days? Your birthday party will be long over by then!

"Kick back and have some lizard stew while you wait," Franklin says. "It's, like, organic."

Guy isn't impressed with this place at all. "They're doing it all wrong!" he tells you angrily, once Franklin has wandered off to take a nap. "If they rigged a proper water collector, maybe tied some snares to catch fresh meat, they wouldn't need to go back for supplies!"

"Sounds like you want to stick around and tell them how it ought to be done," you say.

"I might just do that," says Guy, scratching his chin. "Don't see why we need to go any farther."

Guy might be in his element here, but this isn't how you planned to spend your birthday—eating lizard stew and teaching hippies how to live in the wild. At least you have the promise of a lift out of here in three days' time. Three long, smelly days . . .

Do you want to hang around with Guy and Franklin and wait for the truck to come? Maybe even take a nap? Go to page 34.

If you're impatient, you can always slip off on your own. Go to page 116.

Scarlett sighs. "Hate to say it, but I wish Guy was here. He's better at choppers. Oh well, let's see how much I remember from basic training."

Nervously, you climb in next to her. Scarlett engages the rotors and manages a slightly wobbly takeoff. You clutch the seat as she mutters to herself.

"Watch the torque, Scarlett, watch the torque . . ."

The engine sings. The rotors roar. Gracefully, like a mighty condor taking flight, the helicopter slowly tips over, flies sideways for three seconds, and slams into a tree. It looks like flying a helicopter isn't as easy as Scarlett hoped. The fireball is visible for miles around. Mmmm, crispy explorer!

"Come on, Guy. Let's keep moving. Leave the snakes alone!"

Guy looks sad, but he does as you ask. You set off at a jog once again.

This stone path seems to go on forever. After a while, you pass a tree that looks kind of familiar. You wonder, suddenly, if the path is in a huge circle, and you are just going to keep on running and running without ever reaching safety. That's a frightening thought.

After a couple of hours of running, stopping for water, and running again, you're exhausted.

Guy's flagging, too. "We're going to have to make camp for the night," he says. "What's the first thing we need to do?"

He's testing your survival skills, you realize. "Build a fire?"

"Got it! You go see if you can find some firewood. I'll clear a place for us to sleep."

This is the perfect chance for you to escape! You head off the path, pretending to look for firewood, until Guy's out of sight.

Finally, you're on your own. You're in a dark jungle surrounded by unfamiliar noises, but at least you don't have a thrill-seeking lunatic getting you into trouble anymore. You look up to the stars to get your bearings . . .

. . . and that's when you hear Guy calling your name.

"Hey! Where'd you go? Don't move, OK? It's going to be all right! I'm coming to find you!"

Great. Big-hearted Guy Dangerous thinks you're lost, and he's coming to the rescue. You feel a little bad about running out on him now. Maybe you should pretend you *were* lost, and rejoin him.

If you want to let Guy find you, go to page 46.

If you've made up your mind and you'd rather explore on your own, go to page 116.

You ignore Guy's shouts and grip the rope tight, hoping you don't fall.

The broken bridge swings down and slams against the cliff with the force of a wrecking ball. Shards of wood and stone fly everywhere. The impact knocks the wind out of you, but you still manage to hang on.

Unfortunately, though you keep hold of the rope, the rope doesn't keep hold of the cliff. You look up in horror as the end of the rope comes loose.

The last thing you hear is Guy Dangerous yelling "Noooo!" as you plunge away from his hand—still outstretched—and down toward the waiting rocks. At least your death is quick!

"Hey!" says Guy, poking away with his stick. "It's a nest of snakes! Wish I had something to feed them."

That does it, you decide. Snakes? You hate snakes! You need to get away from Guy Dangerous before he gets you both killed. The only question is whether you wait until nightfall to make your exit, so he'll have less of a chance of stopping you, or whether you just run off the path without looking back, hoping he's distracted by his nest of snakes.

If you slip away now while Guy's poking things with sticks, go to page 116.

If you'd rather wait till night, go to page 29.

You wake up suddenly. Guy is nudging you in the ribs. "Kid, we've got to get out of here, *now.*"

You're in one of the hippie huts. It's dark and smells like rotten old socks. Guy beckons you over to the window.

Outside, Franklin is building something out of wood, singing as he works. You see two poles with rope restraints tied to them. With a lurch of horror, you realize they're meant for you and Guy!

"Listen!" Guy says.

You strain to hear what Franklin's saying: "Dark spirit of the jungle, we're going to feed you well tonight . . . Great prowler, going to give you fresh meat soon . . ."

"He's going to sacrifice us?" you say. "He's crazy!"

"He's been living out here so long, he's lost his mind," Guy says. "I doubt that truck's coming back. Maybe the others bailed on him. Or maybe . . ."

Guy doesn't have to finish that sentence. *Maybe they ended up as sacrifices, too!*

You wonder what the "dark spirit of the jungle"

could be. For a while now, you've been feeling like there's something out there, lurking among the trees.

You try the door. It's barred from the outside.

"Stand back!" Guy tells you. He jumps at the door, crashes right into it, and falls back, wincing in pain. It doesn't break. Outside, Franklin notices the noise, shakes his head, and chuckles.

You look around for a better way out of here. Fortunately, since you're smaller than Guy, you're able to squeeze out the window. You quickly open the front door and let Guy free.

Franklin pounds on a drum. "Dark spirit, come!"

You and Guy turn tail and run, just as something huge comes barging through the trees, bellowing . . .

Keep running all the way to page 40.

You run alongside the river, hoping to see signs of civilization, leaping over boulders and ducking overhanging branches. Nothing you can't handle. You wonder how Scarlett and Guy are doing, wherever they are. To think they were worried about you surviving on your own!

The river empties over a broad waterfall into a lake surrounded by trees. You carefully clamber down the slippery, moss-covered rocks. Sunlight makes rainbows in the mist of the waterfall.

In the middle of the lake is an island bearing a frog-like statue. Mosquitoes buzz in the air. You mentally name this place Frog Falls and wonder if anyone has done so before you.

You sit down beside the lake. It's peaceful here, and for the first time today you stop being annoyed about the birthday party.

Maybe you should stop and rest before moving on? To do this, turn to page 92.

You can see a cavern behind the waterfall, though. To investigate, turn to page 74.

The next day dawns. You wake up to find Guy has already made you breakfast. Somehow he's managed to find eggs.

"I climbed up a tree and there they were," he says, as if it was nothing. "You want some, Smith?"

"Already ate," Montana says and pats his stomach. "Speared me a fish before you got up."

"Fish?"

"From the river up yonder. How's that water bottle of yours holding out?"

You have to grin at these two, carrying on like a pair of squabbling brothers. As the day wears on and you all trek through the jungle together, you feel almost like a family.

You don't reach civilization on the second day. Nor the third, nor the fourth. But you learn more about wilderness life than you ever dreamed. You feel healthier and stronger than you used to.

By the end of your first week in the jungle, it dawns on you that you're not in any hurry to leave after all. You're living like people lived years ago, back in the days of the Wild West—which Montana seems to know a lot about.

You send your parents a postcard to let them know you won't be coming home. They'll probably send a search party sooner or later, but for now you're happy with Guy and Montana. Adios!

You quickly reach the colorful object and skid to a stop. It's a packing crate, lying in the underbrush. You recognize the logo: *ZingyDing Hi-Energy Munchy Bars*. The top's fallen off and you can see hundreds of shiny chocolate bars inside.

"What is *that* doing here?" Scarlett sounds angry. "It's . . . it's not possible!"

Maybe it fell out of a plane, you think. No—it would have smashed. A truck, then? But who would drive out here to the jungle? "One thing's for sure," you tell her. "There are other people here."

"You're not wrong," Scarlett says, pointing at a sticker on the crate. It reads: *STARVING WOLF CATERING*. "I think they work with production companies. Someone's making a film here."

You feel dizzy with relief. "We've got to find them! Let's keep running."

Scarlett nods. "And stock up on Munchy Bars while we're at it. Finders keepers."

Turn to page 60.

40

You and Guy run down the stone path, under a canopy of overhanging branches. The path has crumbled away in places, but you find you can leap over them easily and just keep going.

"Isn't it great to be out in the fresh air, getting plenty of exercise?" Guy says, gasping with the effort of running. "Better than being stuck indoors in front of a computer, huh?" He seems really calm, after what you've just been through. Maybe he actually does have nerves of steel, like he used to say on TV.

"What *was* this place?" you wonder out loud. "I've never heard of ruins like this before."

Guy shrugs. "I guess whoever built this place liked long straight roads. Maybe it was a ritual thing."

From deep in the jungle, far behind you, comes a growl. It's a deep, rattling, hungry sound, like nothing you've ever heard before. "What *is* that?"

"Oh, probably just a bobcat," Guy says, sounding very unsure. "You can't go jumping at shadows if you're going to survive in the wild, you know."

"I think something's following us," you tell him.

Back down the path, there's a heavy crash. Whatever's following you just smashed its way through a whole *tree*. Guy doesn't seem to be taking it seriously.

You speed up a little, leap a lump of masonry, and suddenly see a hideous form up ahead. It's a statue of something like a gorilla, with bulging, muscular arms, one clawed hand held up, and a head like a deformed skull. There's a gaping crack in the stone block it squats on.

Guy comes to a stop in front of it. "That," he says, "is so cool."

You glance back down the path. A flock of birds flies up, squawking in alarm, as something crashes through the trees. "Guy, we need to move!"

"I wonder what this statue is? Looks like Krong, the Bamu-Baku chaos god, but uglier."

Ancient mythology is *not* your main concern right now. You need to get out of this jungle, and fast. Guy's sightseeing tour is slowing you down. Besides, the statue's giving you the creeps. This whole place just feels weird . . . haunted, somehow. Maybe your crash landing wasn't a coincidence?

Now Guy's found a stick and is poking at the crack. "I think there's something alive in here." From inside the stone block comes an angry hiss.

You're feeling impatient now. Guy Dangerous is nice enough, but you're beginning to see why he was fired from his reality TV show.

If you've had enough of Guy's company and want to go it alone, turn to page 33.

But if you choose to stick with Guy, turn to page 46.

43

"We've got to save Zack!" you yell.

But Scarlett's there already. She charges out of the undergrowth at the monster before you can blink. You already know how this is going to end, but it's like a nightmare—you can't look away.

"Get away from him!" Scarlett lets out the kind of screech that attacking battle warriors make in fantasy films. She launches herself at the monster, aiming a perfect kick right at the center of the thing's back.

It connects. The monster goes flying through the air, flailing its arms, lands hard in the middle of the path, rolls over, and looks up at Scarlett.

Angry voices are yelling behind you. "Cut! CUT!"

Farther up the path, Zack Wonder comes to a halt. "What's the problem this time? Boom mike in the shot again?"

A plump little man comes running up. He's furious with Scarlett. "This maniac attacked Jimmy!"

The monster sits up. It pulls off its mask, revealing a rather ill-looking young man. "Lady, that hurt."

Scarlett drops to her knees. "Oh, good heavens. I'm so sorry, I thought . . ."

"You thought he was a real monster?" shouts the little man. "You're nuts! We're trying to film a commercial for running shoes here." This guy must be the director. He snaps his fingers, summoning a solemn-looking man in a suit and glasses. "You've got a lawsuit on your hands, missy."

The rest of the film crew—cameramen, sound

guys, technicians—come and join you, looking annoyed. You listen in and get the idea that Zack was supposed to be running from a creepy monster through the jungle. *That* was someone's idea of a good commercial? Maybe they were planning to make it look cooler with lots of computer graphics.

In the end, Zack steps in and calms everyone down. "The young lady was trying to save my life," he says, "so let's not give her too hard a time, huh?"

"Thanks, Zack." Scarlett grins, her cheeks pink.

Turn to page 71 to see what happens next.

Much, much later, you're sitting across the campfire from Guy. You're bone-tired, but you really don't want to sleep. There are scary noises coming from the jungle all around you, and you keep thinking you see shapes moving in the shadows.

"Wish I had my guitar," Guy says. He pokes the fire with the toe of his boot. "Nothing makes the night go by like a sing-along."

The next moment, you see a shadowy figure walking steadily out of the jungle. It moves silently and quickly until it's right behind Guy.

"Guy! Behind you!"

"Huh? What's that—"

"Lucky for you I ain't a bandit, nor one of them crazy monkey-worshippers," says a harsh voice. "You two would've been sliced open quick as spit."

The man—you can see it's a man now—squats down by your fire. He's dusty, wearing a hat and shirt, and has stubble even scruffier than Guy's.

"Nah, I knew you were there," Guy says easily.

"If you'd tried anything, I'd have taken you down."

The man snorts. "With this?"

He throws Guy's machete in front of him. You wonder how he managed to take it without Guy noticing.

"No, smart guy, with these!" Guy angrily holds up his fists. "Who the heck are you, anyway?"

The man tips his hat and gives you half a grin. "Name's Smith. Montana Smith. Explorer."

Guy laughs like he can't believe it. "The so-called second-greatest explorer of all time?"

"That's me."

"Reckon you must have gotten yourself as lost as a penguin in the desert, then. You were lucky to run into us." Guy spits into the fire. It sizzles.

You're curious. "How come you're here in the jungle?"

"Relics," says Montana Smith. He raps his knuckles on the flagstone beneath you. "This here's the ruins of a city, and it ain't in any history book. There's riches here no man's laid eyes on since before the comin' of Cortez."

Montana's voice is like gravel. He talks to you about the stone paths that crisscross the jungle, while Guy stiffly fetches his machete back and whittles some wood into pointed stakes. "To make snares," he eventually explains.

"Snares?" Montana laughs. "Are you too chicken to hunt with spears?"

"Maybe you and me can do a little hunting tomorrow, Mr. Smith," Guy fires back. "We'll see who bags the most meat. Sound good, cowboy?"

Montana lies back and pulls his hat down over his eyes. "Sure. Let's get some shut-eye, kid. Your, ah, *friend* here can take first watch."

"Jerk," Guy mutters. He tosses a half-whittled stake over his shoulder into the dark.

You lie down and close your eyes, but your mind

is racing. You need to get out of this jungle, back to civilization, and to your birthday party. It sounds like both Montana Smith and Guy Dangerous are more interested in proving they can survive out here in the wilderness! You could probably learn a lot if you stuck around, but you might be here for a while.

Also, they are kind of turning this into a competition. When it's your turn to go on watch, you could just slip away on your own and leave them to it.

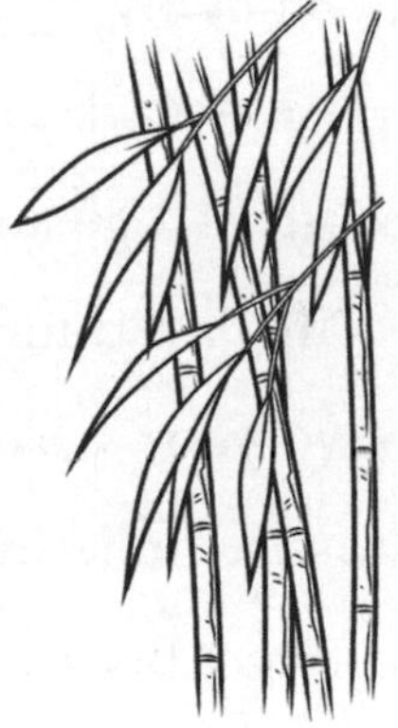

If you want to stay with Montana and Guy, go to page 37.

If you'd rather sneak off while you have the chance, go to page 116.

You've barely taken a few steps when Zack Wonder, world-famous football player, comes charging up the path. A camera crew is following behind him, filming everything he does.

He tackles you without thinking—you're an unexpected obstacle in his way, after all—and you both go tumbling off the path.

Unfortunately, some of the plant life in this jungle is still unknown to science. There are species of Venus flytrap here that could swallow a horse. You and Zack tumble directly into the gaping green mouth of a gigantic carnivorous plant.

The last thing you see is the plant's jaws closing above your head. The last thing you hear is Zack Wonder hollering the kind of language that would never get broadcast on national television.

The bad news is you're both dead; the good news is the cameras were still rolling, and you're the star of the most viral Internet video ever!

"Good choice," says Scarlett. "Here, take this. In case we get separated." From her bag, she passes you a small compass.

Make a note that you've got this. It's important.

"You know, primitive man did just fine without all those doodads," Guy says.

"Well, if primitive man can't find his way back to camp, he can always send up a distress flare." Scarlett tosses Guy a flare. He scowls, but tucks it into his belt.

You wave. Guy gives you an awkward grin. "Good luck, kid. Stay out of trouble."

Scarlett's already moving, heading off into the jungle, her long legs pumping. You hurry after her. It's strange—you've always thought survival was about *saving* your energy, but Scarlett's treating this as if it were a race!

The ground here is boggy, with dry parts that you have to jump on. You've barely been leaping for five minutes before you come across a stone walkway, raised off the jungle floor by blocks.

"There it is!" yelps Scarlett.

"You were expecting that?" you gasp.

"I, uh, saw it when we were crashing," Scarlett says. "It stood out against all the green."

One after the other, you bound onto the walkway. It must be part of an ancient ruin, but it's in pretty good shape, considering.

You run alongside Scarlett, enjoying the firmer ground, and suddenly the two of you break out of the forest. Bright sunlight dazzles your eyes.

The walkway extends out over a dry, stony gorge. It must have been a bridge once, but now there's a wide gap in the middle, way too far to jump. On the far side, you can see the crumbled stump of the other end. There's an interesting-looking cave mouth beneath it.

Maybe it's a tomb.

Scarlett staggers to a halt. "Blast. That's put a damper on things."

You glance down over the edge. Are those white rocks way down there, or bleached bones? You can't tell.

Scarlett's rummaging in her bag. "We've got two choices, kid . . . figure out how to get across, or go back the way we came."

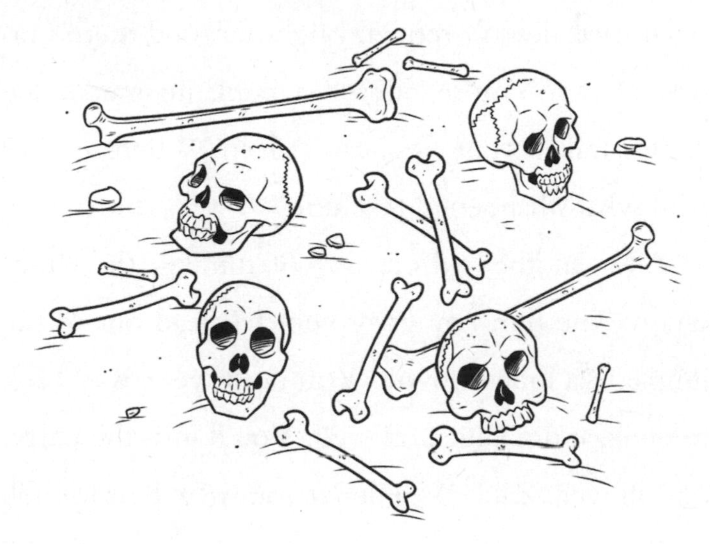

To turn around and head back into the jungle, turn to page 57.

To try to cross the bridge somehow, turn to page 67.

You have a great time with the film crew. Zack even invites you to spend your next birthday at his mansion in Hollywood. The director films a few more takes of Zack running through the jungle, pursued by a (now recovered) Jimmy in his monster costume. Even he seems happy.

Scarlett doesn't return. Night falls and there's no sign of her. You're offered a bunk in one of the crew's trailers, but you can't sleep. Where *is* she? And what's happened to Guy?

After another whole day of filming, the shoot wraps. The film company vehicles head out of the jungle in a long convoy. You're on your way back to civilization, alive and well. You'll miss the party, but oh well. Zack Wonder is your new best friend!

But unanswered questions still haunt you—did Guy make it out of the jungle alive, and what was Scarlett really up to? Maybe other paths hold the answers . . .

You and Scarlett dive into the undergrowth. A damp green fern frond dangles in your face. Neither of you makes a sound.

What happens next makes your eyes widen in shock. A tall, hefty man in a football uniform comes charging down the jungle path. From the number on his chest, you recognize him immediately.

"That's Zack Wonder!" you shout.

Zack's arms and legs pump as he runs past you. You wonder what on earth a top-ranked football player is doing here in the depths of the jungle.

A second later, you find out. He's running away from the *thing* that's following him.

The beast chasing Zack has the green warty skin of a toad but the fanged mouth of an alligator and leathery ears like a bat's. Bulging eyes roll around in its head as it runs past you.

Turn to page 43.

You and Scarlett run side by side, weaving in and out of the trees. It's actually kind of beautiful here, you think. Exotic plants tower over you, their blooms open like alien mouths. Rainbow-colored birds in the trees ruffle their feathers. Slanted rays of sunlight shine down between the overhanging branches. Apart from the stone blocks you sometimes see, there's no sign that anyone has been here in hundreds of years. If you hadn't crash-landed, this might be a cool outing.

Just as you're beginning to enjoy yourself, a beast-like roar rings out behind you. Scarlett gasps. You don't want to look over your shoulder, but you do anyway. You catch a glimpse of a hulking creature, black and menacing, far in the distance.

"So, the legends were true," says Scarlett, picking up speed. "Whatever you do, don't stop!"

Off to your right, through the trees, you see a flash of bright color. It looks man-made, not natural.

To investigate that color, go to page 39.

To keep running, turn to page 60.

You and Guy sneak through the jungle, closing in on the column of red smoke. You're not moving very fast, but you're not making much noise, either. You wonder if whoever set the smoke off will still be there when you reach it.

Eventually, you come within sight of a clearing where an ugly statue stands. The smoke is coming from a canister on top of it. Guy is about to run ahead when you stop him and make a *shush* gesture.

You've just seen Scarlett Fox lurking behind a tree, holding a small black device in her hand. Guy's eyes widen as he sees it.

"That's a proximity-mine trigger," he whispers. "She's trying to set a trap for us! The whole clearing must be mined."

"Sneaky," you say. "I bet she was planning to trap us, then bargain for the idol."

"Well, we've got the drop on her!" Guy grins wolfishly. "Shall we?"

Together you advance on Scarlett, who hasn't noticed you. You get ready to rush her . . . and then

Guy steps on a twig. She spins around, alarmed.

"What's wrong?" you scoff. "Not expecting us?"

"I . . ." she blusters. "It's . . . it's not what it looks like!"

Just as it looks like things are about to get really ugly, the familiar roar of a demon monkey echoes through the jungle.

Run to page 122.

The path widens out into a clearing. People have been here very recently. You can tell this partly from the tire tracks on the ground and the trampled plants, but mostly from the trailer the size of a small house that's still parked here.

Excitement grips you. It looks like your ride back to civilization is here! Maybe you can still make it to your birthday party.

The next second, you hear that strange roar again, and shouting voices. Your skin runs cold.

Uh-oh. Quick—hide!

To hide in the nearby trampled foliage, run to page 55.

To dart across the clearing to hide in the trailer, run to page 50.

Guy grins. "Good choice, kid. We'll see you later, Scarlett. Don't get lost, now."

Scarlett's already pulling her backpack on. "You'd just have slowed me down anyway, Mr. Dangerous," she says wryly.

The next moment, she's off, running into the jungle as if this was a high school track meet.

Guy shakes his head. "She'll be sending up a distress flare before sundown, just you wait."

You're not so sure. Scarlett's clearly good at taking care of herself. Perhaps a little *too* good.

"Let's get going," Guy says. "We've got a lot of ground to cover. Oh, and take this. It'll help when the vines get thicker."

He gives you a small machete inscribed with his initials.

Make a note that you've got Guy's machete. This is important.

Together, you and Guy move off through the thick jungle greenery. You follow a thin trail that winds in and out through the trees. You can't tell if people made it, or how long ago.

Strange noises come to your ears—the squawking of distant birds, the buzz of insects, the rustle of unseen animals in the undergrowth.

"First step in survival is to get our bearings," Guy says. "Sun's over there, so that's the west. Scarlett headed off to the north, so we'll head due south."

His confidence makes you feel better about all this. You speed up a little. Next thing you know, you trip and fall forward.

Guy catches your arm. "Hey, watch out for the roots!"

"Do we have to go so slow?" you complain.

"Go as fast as you like, just don't wear yourself out. You want to run? Let's run. Just jump and duck when I say to!"

This is more like it. You and Guy go bounding through the jungle, leaping over roots and ducking branches. You soon get into a rhythm. This isn't so hard!

Suddenly, your feet are pounding on hard, weathered stone, not soft, spongy earth.

"It's a path!" Guy yells. "A real man-made one. We have to see where this goes!"

Up ahead, the path splits in two. Left or right?

To go left, where you can hear rushing water and see bright daylight, go to page 18.

To go right, where the path leads deeper into the jungle, go to page 40.

You fly a little way toward the cave mouth, but not nearly far enough. You catch a brief glimpse of the golden idol that squats inside, grinning as if it were mocking you.

Then you plummet several hundred feet and vanish beneath the river's surface, never to come up . . . *Glub glub!*

Scarlett reluctantly slides over and lets you climb into the pilot's seat. She doesn't look happy about this. In fact, if you didn't know better, you'd think she was angry.

Brushing off her concern, you engage the rotors and gently ease back the joystick.

Fortunately, you manage to fly the helicopter more or less level. Soon you're rising above the trees. You've got your ticket out of there!

But then you see what looks like a film crew down below, yelling and waving at you. The sound of the rotors must have brought them running.

If you keep going until you're clear of the jungle, go to page 133.

If you think it would be a better idea to land and introduce yourselves, go to page 71.

Scarlett tricked you! You jump—and go falling forward into a square pit, mostly hidden by the jungle foliage. You grab at the edge, but it's too late. Next second, you crash down into a matted tangle of old creepers. Pain shoots up your leg.

Scarlett peers down at you from above. "I'm really sorry I had to do that," she sighs, shaking her head. "You're too tough for your own good. I never thought you'd last this long in the jungle. To be honest, I expected you to wait around to be rescued!"

You struggle to your feet, but your leg hurts too badly to stand. "Help me out of here!" you yell.

"Sorry, I can't have company where I'm going. Adios! It's been fun." She gives you a little wave, then runs off.

Maybe you should pursue her. Your leg aches, but you could try climbing one of the creepers dangling into the pit. Go to page 70.

On the other hand, your leg hurts pretty badly. To wait in the pit and hope someone rescues you, turn to page 83.

"What have you got in mind?" you ask Scarlett.

"Zip-line!"

Scarlett produces a short pistol-like device with a grappling hook on the end. She takes aim and fires at the far side of the broken bridge. Again, you wonder what secrets are hidden in the cave below that stony stump.

The hook, trailing a rope, launches over the chasm and snags in the bricks. Scarlett checks it's secure, then fastens this end using pitons.

OK, this is crazy. Scarlett Fox is well prepared, sure. But it's a little strange that she packed a *grappling hook* with the rest of her gadgets. It's almost as though she was expecting this.

"You know how to use one of these?" she asks.

"Sure."

She passes you a metal clip, which you click onto the taut rope. All you need to do is launch yourself over the edge, and you'll whizz across to the other side.

"Want me to go first?" Scarlett offers.

"No, I've got this." You figure it'll be easiest if you get this done quickly.

You take a deep breath and push yourself out. You go whizzing down the zip-line. It's exciting! Then you notice a gleam of gold inside the cave.

You need to make a lightning-fast decision.

Do you let go of the zip-line just before the end, to try to land in the cave mouth?
Go to page 64.

If you hang on all the way to be sure of reaching the other side, turn to page 15.

You work your way back up to daylight through a narrow, root-choked tunnel.

Up ahead, you see the outline of a stone pyramid through the trees. You run toward it and hear the sound of fighting.

Run on to page 103.

With a lot of effort, you manage to scramble out of the pit. By the time you reach the top, it's getting dark and Scarlett is long gone. Luckily, your leg doesn't hurt so badly anymore.

There's nothing for it but to head deeper into the jungle and see if you can pick up Scarlett's trail.

Turn to page 116.

Thankfully, the misunderstanding is soon forgotten, and everybody calms down once Zack Wonder steps in. Everyone always says he's a heck of a nice guy in person. Now you know it's true. Even two strangers interrupting his incredibly important film shoot doesn't make him grouchy.

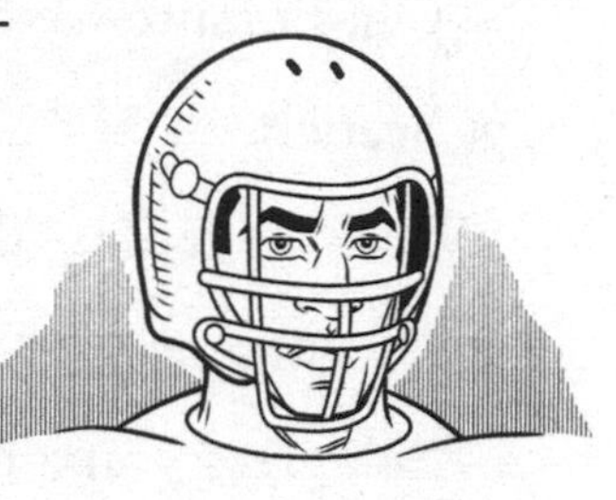

You spend some time hanging out with the film crew, who is super cool. You ask if any of them have seen Guy Dangerous out in the wild, but nobody has. A few of them think they've seen strange creatures lurking off the path, though—"like a huge monkey with a skull for a head."

The more you learn about this jungle, the stranger the place seems.

Zack Wonder is sorry to hear about the plane crash. "You're welcome to hang with us," he says. "We're not leaving until the shoot's done, though, so you'll have to wait for a lift."

"Oh, I'm sure we can work together for a while," says Scarlett.

Work together for how long, you wonder? You've got a *party* to get to, or did she forget?

Zack gives you a brand-new pair of the sneakers he's promoting. "If you're going to run, run with the best!" he says.

You eagerly put them on. Suddenly, missing the party doesn't seem so bad. Eating burgers in the jungle with a multi-millionaire football player is a pretty cool substitute!

"Happy birthday, kid," Zack says, patting you on the back and knocking the wind out of you.

"Hey, Zack, I had a thought," says Scarlett, looking sly. "I heard there's a ruined temple somewhere in this jungle."

"So?"

"Wouldn't it make a perfect location to shoot your commercial in? You'd look great running down those mysterious old paths."

"Sounds good." Zack shrugs. "Lead the way."

"I'm not sure where it is exactly," Scarlett says. "Perhaps if I go scout it out? I'll come back and let you know when I've found it." She turns to you and adds, "I guess you'll want to stay here with Zack, right?"

Yet again, you mull over how much Scarlett already seems to know about this jungle. She seems crazy-keen to find this mysterious temple of hers. Maybe the temple is the real reason you're here!

If you choose to wait with the film crew and Zack Wonder until Scarlett returns, go to page 54.

If you want to head out with her and look for the temple together, go to page 76.

But you're beginning to mistrust Scarlett. If you want to slip away and look for the temple on your own, go to page 116.

You find yourself in a huge, dark, underground cave. It's flooded with water that looks freezing cold, and the air has a damp mineral smell. From the cavern roof dangle hundreds of creepers, roots, and vines, like an upside-down forest.

You're standing on a narrow, gravelly bank at the water's edge. You poke a toe experimentally into the water. Instantly, white shapes lunge at your foot and you whip it back. The water's full of stubby little fish. Is there such a thing as the Blind Cave Piranha?

How will you get across this underground lake? An idea strikes you. You grab a dangling creeper and start to climb it. Then you swing and grab another. Cool—it works! By swinging from creeper to creeper, you're able to stay clear of the water and the hungry little fish. You swing and grab, swing and grab until you see daylight up ahead! Not far now.

To grab a thick green creeper and make one final swing, turn to page 80.

To make several swings on thinner-looking creepers, turn to page 69.

You swerve to the left and narrowly avoid falling into an overgrown pit, which was almost invisible in the half-light. Missed it by *that* much.

"Blast it! You just don't quit, do you?" Scarlett shouts and runs off.

She *deliberately* told you to jump the wrong way, you realize! She's trying to shake you off.

You set off in pursuit, but she's sprinting as if her life depended on it. Both of you weave in and out, dodging piles of stone and leaping cracks in the ground. It's a close-run thing, but eventually Scarlett gets away. You gasp for breath and try to get your bearings.

You have no clue where you are. All around is thick jungle.

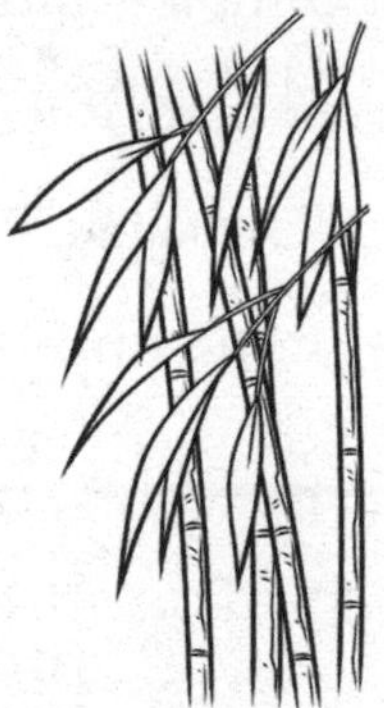

Turn to page 116.

Scarlett stares at you. "Are you sure? Looking for the temple might be dangerous . . ."

"Sounds like fun," you say firmly.

Scarlett narrows her eyes. In that moment, you know she's hiding something. And you know that she *knows* that you know.

Then she's all smiles again. "Let's go!"

Soon, you and Scarlett are running down the seemingly endless jungle paths. You cross stone bridges and pass through short tunnels that smell as if bats have nested in them.

"Where's the temple supposed to be?" you ask.

"According to legend, this whole ruined city is the temple," she gasps. "We need to find the most sacred part of it. The place where they hid the . . ."

"The what?"

"Look out! JUMP TO YOUR RIGHT!"

If you heed Scarlett's warning and jump to your right, run to page 66.

If you ignore her and run to your left, turn to page 75.

You hang on, hoping the bird will just go away. But it doesn't.

Instead, something terrible happens. The bird's squawks and flaps attract the attention of a dark shape that comes loping out of the forest above. You are unable to do anything but look up in horror as it grins and hefts a boulder at you. At least you left your mark on the world.

A saw blade whizzes up through the ground, and you dodge . . . right into it.

Um. It's best if we don't go into detail. Maybe that second leg was holding you back anyway!

The slope down to the river is far steeper than you thought. You climb down the jagged rocks, taking it slowly, a step at a time. In places, you have to hang on with your hands and feet, clinging to handholds and toeholds. You're not scared of heights, are you?

Slowly, carefully, you edge your way toward the water. You're halfway down when a stab of pain shoots through your head. Brightly colored wings buffet your face. Some weird exotic bird, like a cross between a parrot and a heron, is attacking you! It just pecked you hard with its sharp beak, and it's about to do it again.

This is *bad*. You can't climb safely with this stupid bird in your face! It's hard enough to cling on as it is.

You could let go with one of your hands and try to fend the bird off. Turn to page 84.

To cling to the cliff face and hope the bird goes away, turn to page 77.

Your fingers clutch cool, scaly flesh. The "creeper" raises its head and hisses furiously at you. It's a giant anaconda!

You both plunge into the water. Leathery coils surround you. After a frantic struggle, you're suddenly able to free yourself. Gasping, you wade out of the lake and toward the light. How did you possibly survive that?

You turn and look over your shoulder, and see the blind cave piranhas tucking into the enormous snake. So that's what happened. Kind of disgusting, but at least you're alive.

Run on to page 69.

"Hey, wait a minute. Don't be too hasty." Guy reaches out, but you're already striding away.

"Send us a postcard!" Scarlett shouts. "Don't talk to any strange monkeys!"

Her teasing just makes you all the more certain that this is the right thing to do. You're feeling pretty cranky about missing your birthday party. You forge ahead into the jungle alone, determined to reach civilization before Guy *or* Scarlett.

You fall into a sort of jogging run, fast enough to cover the ground, but not so fast that you can't duck out of the way of low branches or leap over tangled roots. Within minutes, you're out of sight of the crash site. This is it. You're on your own, in the wild, miles from anywhere.

You run and run and run. Light starts to stream through the jungle canopy as the trees thin out. You notice you're coming to a rocky area with less vegetation. Soon you hear rushing water.

Up ahead, the ground slopes down steeply.

You're sure that that way leads to a river.

You remember that settlements are often built near water, so following the river might be a good move. Then again, wild animals come down to the water, too, don't they?

To your left you can see what looks like a stone pathway, half-buried in the spongy jungle floor. It must be part of a ruin.

To clamber down the slope and try to follow the river, go to page 79.

To take the path deeper into the jungle, go to page 90.

You wait . . . and wait, and wait. Nobody comes. Years later, explorers discover your skeleton. You end up in a museum, which isn't quite the party you were hoping for!

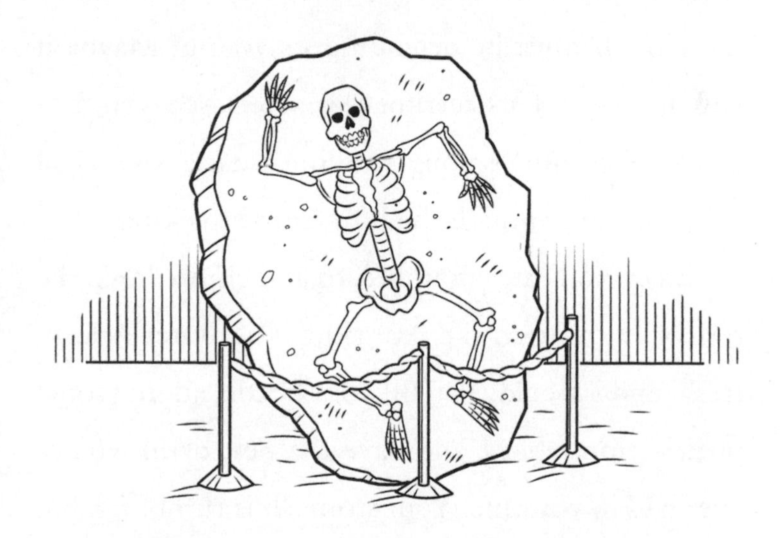

You swipe at the bird, hanging on desperately with the other hand. "Shoo!" you say. "Go away!"

Your flailing seems to make it angrier. As you endure the bird's buffeting, you notice a nest along the cliff. It must be defending its young! Maybe if you get out of its territory, it won't see you as a threat. You shuffle along, moving as far away as you can, and sure enough the bird stops attacking.

Phew. You catch your breath and climb down the rest of the way to the riverside. The water's clean, fresh, and icy cold. You fill your bottle, adding some purification tablets, and have the best drink you've ever had in your life. Your stomach is rumbling, but you don't have much food on you. Better to save it until you really need it.

You follow the course of the river. Soon you find yourself by a riverside shrine to some strange local spirit. A carved wooden statue squats inside. Offerings of fruit have been left here—which must mean there are people nearby!

Your stomach rumbles again. Loudly.

Maybe you should leave an offering of food, too, just for good luck and to show respect. If you believe in that sort of thing.

On the other hand, there's a lot of fresh fruit here and the spirit's not going to eat it, is it? Food is food and it looks delicious. Why let it go to waste?

To leave some food yourself, even though it will mean you go hungry, go to page 87.

To eat the offerings, turn to page 89.

To ignore the shrine and follow the river, turn to page 36.

You're glad you have some matches from when Guy and Scarlett distributed the survival gear. You manage to get some kindling lit, and soon a column of smoke rises high into the sky.

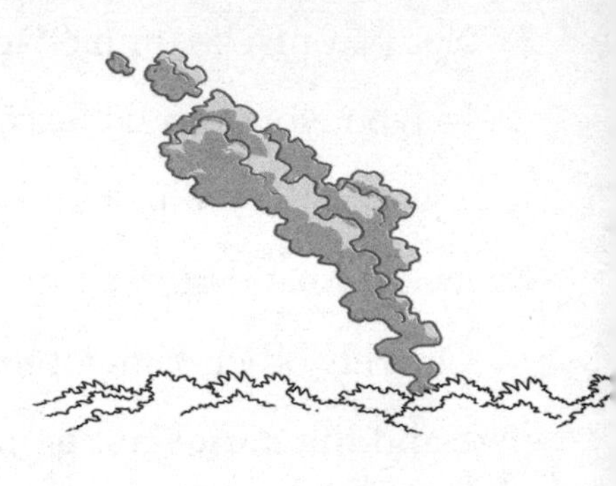

Before long, people find you. Your happiness is short-lived when you see their weapons and their unpleasant grins. They're bandits, hoping to find some helpless traveler stranded out here. As you're bundled into their jeep and driven to their hideout, you wonder if you'll ever see your family again.

Fortunately, your family and friends raise enough for your ransom and you are set free. You go on every talk show, you're in all the papers, and your book about your experiences is an instant best seller. You missed out on that birthday party, though . . .

Feeling a little silly, you leave some of your precious food supply at the shrine. The wooden statue starts to move. For a horrible second, you think it's coming to life. Then it falls over.

Warily, you approach. The fallen statue has revealed an opening in the cliff face, just big enough for you to crawl down. Was the statue trying to help, somehow? You shake your head. That's silly!

You only have a bit of food left now. You check your pockets, hoping to find some forgotten crumb left in there. To your amazement, you find a strange golden berry. It must have fallen into your pocket from a plant by the wayside. But you haven't *seen* any plants with berries. You eat it anyway. It's delicious, and you feel as if you've eaten a whole meal.

The statue is grinning. Was it grinning before? Look at that, you've broken out in goose bumps. You shake off the creepy feeling and crawl into the opening. Soon you're descending rough steps, down to a flooded cavern.

Run on to page 74.

A rusty saw blade nearly slices through you, but you dodge the right way and avoid it. *So* close. So that's how the skeleton lost his leg!

Run on to page 99.

The fruit tastes delicious, but suddenly you start to cough and choke. Your skin turns gray all over. You feel your arms and legs stiffen, forcing you into a crouching posture. A fixed grin spreads over your face . . .

Before a minute has passed, you have been completely transformed into a second statue, condemned to watch over the shrine alongside the first one. Looks like you're stuck here for a while! Oh well, at least it's a job. And you get to eat fresh fruit every single day.

90

The stone path twists sharply to the right and then to the left. You swerve around the corners, then dive out of the way of a long spear that thrusts up from below. A trap!

If you weren't so quick on your feet, you would have been impaled like a sausage on a stick. Just as you're congratulating yourself, a sharp *crack* warns you that another trap has gone off.

Oof!

You duck and roll out of the way of the blade that whizzes through the space where you were half a second ago.

Maybe you'd be safer off the path. You look over the edge and see that the jungle floor here is moving. The whole area is crawling with bugs, and some of them look venomous.

On second thought, the path is fine after all. On the ground up ahead, you notice a skeleton.

A *human* skeleton.

Uh-oh. What's your next move?

You can run back the other way and climb down the rocky slope to the river instead.
Run to page 79.

Or you can run ahead, dodging to the right.
Turn to page 88.

Or run ahead, dodging to the left.
Turn to page 78.

You fall asleep . . . and wake up to find yourself covered with gigantic, bloated mosquitoes the size of hummingbirds. Wow. They grow them big out here. Fortunately, you're not conscious for very long. All that blood-sucking is just unsanitary!

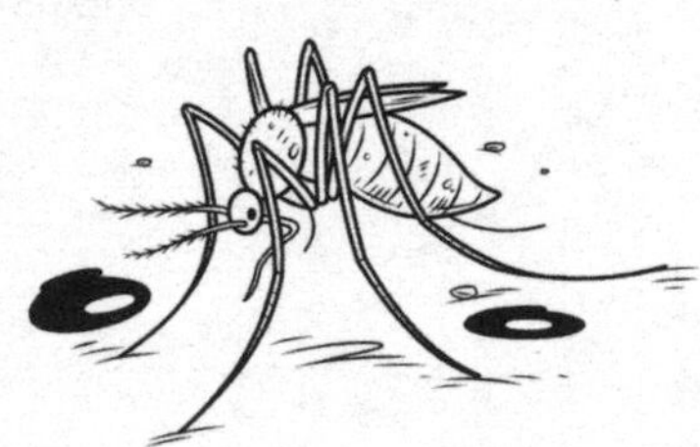

"Careful," whispers Karma. "It stinks in here. Might be some sort of lair."

She's right. The heavy stench of animal fur and filth is strong here. Karma shines a flashlight around and you see the cavern is full of extremely creepy stone statues. They look like bigger, uglier versions of the golden idol you're carrying.

You step forward and something cracks under your foot. It's a bone. The floor is littered with them. "I think this is where the demon monkeys hang out," you whisper. "When they're not chasing us."

You tense up, expecting a huge demon monkey—or a swarm of little ones—to come rushing out of the darkness. But nothing moves. "I don't think they're home," Karma says.

Then something catches your eye that isn't a bone or a piece of ancient carving. It's a modern laptop computer, smashed to bits. Karma's flashlight shines on other objects: a clipboard, a backpack, a set of climbing gear.

For a second, you think you'll find what's left of

Scarlett here, too. But then you realize this isn't her stuff. It's all stamped with the same corporate logo, a sign like a diamond with an eye in it.

"Something deeply weird is going on," you tell Karma. "Other people have been here recently. Look at the quality of their gear."

Karma passes you something she's found. "I think you need to see this."

It's a folded, printed document. By flashlight, you open it up. It has a picture—an old black-and-white picture—of the very idol you're carrying. Below the picture are instructions for "Team Delta" to establish a meeting point in the jungle, so that "Agent Renarde" can deliver the idol, which is "estimated to be worth billions."

"Who is Agent Renarde?" you wonder.

Karma looks thoughtful. "*Renard* is the French word for 'fox' . . ."

And all of a sudden, you know. You head back out and run toward the brightly lit jungle area.

Run on to page 102.

The floor gives way beneath you, and you tumble down into a flooded cavern. Man down! But by some miracle, you're unhurt.

Run to page 74.

It's a tremendous view from up here. You can see for miles . . . and a search party could probably see you. You couldn't wish for a better place to signal from.

There's some dry timber nearby that you could use to start a signal fire. It might take a while, though . . . You don't relish the thought of being stuck up here for ages trying to keep a fire going long enough to attract attention.

Still, it might be the only chance you've got of being rescued.

To try to start a signal fire, run to page 86.

To climb back down and visit the pyramid instead, go to page 103.

You and Karma walk into the camp. The bright spotlights dazzle your eyes. Nobody shouts a warning or comes running up to confront you. It seems like this place is deserted.

"Spooky, isn't it?" Karma says. "Where do you suppose they went?"

"Maybe the demon monkeys got them," you guess.

You and Karma explore the base. You find plenty of food and water, all in sealed packs like military rations. In one tent you find a mission briefing. It tells you that this base camp is where Scarlett Fox was supposed to hand over the idol you're carrying, to a bunch of scary-sounding corporate thugs! A recent note reveals they've gone to search the temple, since Scarlett hasn't shown up with the idol yet.

"Our plane crash was all a ruse!" you tell Karma. "Scarlett's company set the whole thing up so she could steal the idol."

"Looks like the plan blew up in their faces," says Karma. "You've got the idol and Scarlett's gone."

When you look in the largest tent, you see sleeping bags laid out on comfortable-looking air beds. You've been running for almost a whole day and a night now. The thought of a few hours' rest is almost too tempting for words. Karma looks like she's longing for a sleep, too.

"I say we eat their food, sleep in their beds, and move on," Karma says. "Call it Operation Goldilocks. They deserve it."

If you take the opportunity to eat and sleep, go to page 105.

To sneak off through the jungle, go to page 144.

The path slopes gradually upward. Then, with no warning at all, you see a view that stops you in your tracks. You've reached the ruins of a city that was swallowed up by the jungle hundreds of years ago. Stone paths like the one you're on wind in and out of low stone dwellings and crumbling towers. Here and there are statues of strange beings with animal faces. The walls are decorated with stone carvings showing twining leaves and angry-looking people with tusk-like teeth.

You try to remember if you've ever heard of a lost city in this part of the world before, but nothing comes to mind. Maybe it's been kept secret all this time. You can't be the first outsider to discover it . . . can you?

Even though it's an amazing sight, it's not helping you get out of this jungle. It's civilization, but not the sort you were hunting for!

Maybe if you climb higher, you could get a better view of the land. You look around for places where you could climb.

You see a stepped pyramid a little way away and a tower closer to you. The tower almost reaches up past the treetops.

If you head to the pyramid, turn to page 103.

If you climb the tower, go to page 96.

To poke around among the rubble closer to where you are, go to page 95.

"Hey!" you shout. "Over here, you skull-headed jerks!"

The demon monkeys instantly notice. They all look at you and freeze for a second. Then they charge at you, screeching. You gulp and get ready for a fight. The young woman gives you a grin that says *thanks*, cracks her neck, and comes to help you.

Disgusting, furry bodies leap up and clutch at you. You fend them off as best you can, but there are too many demon monkeys, and they're just too fast. You console yourself with the knowledge that you are about to die a hero's death . . . buried under a huge pile of crazy demon monkeys.

Through the jungle you can see spotlights mounted on tripods and large tents set up. This is clearly a base of some sort, but for whom? Perhaps the eye-in-diamond symbol on the tent walls is a clue.

You don't see any movement. There's no light in the tents. Perhaps the people who set this place up are away. Or perhaps they're lying in ambush.

Someone has hacked a path through the jungle greenery. It's the obvious way into the base.

"Do we go in through the front," Karma Lee whispers to you, "or sneak around the side?"

If you want to follow the path straight in, go to page 97.

To stealthily look for another way in, go to page 144.

You clamber up the huge steps of the pyramid. Yells, grunts, thwacks, and thumps come from up there. Sounds like a fight is going on!

When you reach the top, you see a bizarre sight. A young Asian woman is fighting for her life against a horde of hideous demon monkeys. They don't have real monkey heads, just the bare skulls of some other animal altogether. They leap at her, clawing at her face, only to be driven back by expertly placed kicks and punches.

The strength in her legs is amazing—she's kicking the creatures over the treetops! But the more demon monkeys she bashes through the air, the more seem to rush at her, swarming up the pyramid.

She's using some kind of martial art you've never seen before, a strange flowing blend of styles. She's clearly an amazing fighter, but it looks like there are just too many demon monkeys for her to cope with. If she doesn't get help to fight them, she might go down. And you're the only one here.

You're tired and hungry, though. Not the best time to take on a pack of demon monkeys. Perhaps you shouldn't join a fight you might not be able to win. You could always try something different, like distracting them. That might give her an edge?

If you want to charge in and help the woman by fighting alongside her, run to page 108.

If you want to help by distracting the demon monkeys so she can escape, turn to page 101.

To sneak off and hope the demon monkeys don't notice you, turn to page 107.

You stuff yourself on the food in the ration packs. Any other day, it would taste like cardboard and soup powder. Right now it's a feast. You snuggle up in a sleeping bag and are asleep in seconds.

Next thing you know, you're being shaken awake. "On your feet!" says a gruff voice.

Two burly guards pull you out of the sleeping bag. They're wearing combat gear and goggles. Looks like they came back early. You shove them away and get to your feet, still woozy from the sleep you were enjoying seconds ago.

Scarlett Fox strides into the tent. "*Where is it?*"

"Where's what?"

"Don't play games!" she says furiously. "The idol you took from the temple. Hand it over!"

"Oh, you mean this?" You pull the idol from the sleeping bag, where you'd stashed it. The guards step back, as if they think it's dangerous.

Scarlett smiles, looking friendly again. "I'm going to need you to be all grown-up and sensible now. Pass the idol to me, and everything will be just fine. We'll all fly home together and put this silly misunderstanding behind us."

Where, you wonder, is Karma Lee? Did they capture her, too? Or did she make it out of the base? Why didn't she wake you before these goons came back?

"I'm running out of patience," says Scarlett, still grinning.

If you hand over the idol and surrender,
go to page 143.

If you push past her and run from the tent,
trusting that Karma is out there somewhere,
turn to page 147.

As you sneak off, the demon monkeys notice you. They abandon the woman and swarm over you instead, recognizing an easier lunch when they see one. Congratulations—you're tasty *and* nutritious, which counts as an accomplishment. *Nom nom!*

"Hey, lady! Need a hand?"

You run and stand back-to-back with the young woman. Skull-headed demon monkeys come flying at you from all sides, hissing and swiping. You punch, kick, and fling for all you're worth. The monkeys land a few painful scratches, but together, you and the woman stand your ground against them.

You soon find that your fighting styles work in perfect harmony. Every time you miss a blow, she's there with a strike of her own. Whenever the demon monkeys overwhelm her, you're able to thin their numbers.

After what seems like an eternity, a beast-like roar echoes out across the ruined city. All the demon monkeys turn and flee as one, scampering down the sides of the pyramid.

Before she says a word, the woman lifts a talisman from around her neck and places it around yours. It shows a yin-yang design, but it's made out

of some weird holographic glass. The talisman swirls and rotates as you look at it. *Remember that you have the talisman—this will be important later on.*

"Karma Lee," the woman says, shaking your hand. "A true pleasure to meet you. I suggest we join forces."

"I was thinking the same thing!" For some reason, you feel you can trust Karma Lee.

"You're quite the fighter," she says.

"You too. What was that martial art you were using?" you ask.

"I . . . don't think you'd know it," Karma says carefully. "It's a little ahead of your time." She glances over her shoulder. "Not to be rude, but we need to run. It's coming."

"What's coming?"

"That!"

You see a gigantic skull-headed demon monkey leaping from stone platform to stone platform. It's definitely coming your way.

Run to page 112.

110

Together, you and Guy race through the jungle, heading for the column of red smoke.

"Do you think it's Scarlett?" you ask.

"Probably," Guy says. "She could be hurt, or could've found help. Or someone could be using one of her smoke canisters. Be ready for anything."

Not long after, you find the source of the smoke. It's pouring from a canister stuck on top of a leering statue of a man clutching his ears and sticking his tongue out. There's nothing else here but the remains of a campfire.

Guy frowns. "Scarlett?" he yells. "Where are you?"

Scarlett steps out from behind a tree twenty feet away. "Right here." She holds up a small device that flashes and beeps. "Don't move, either of you."

"Aww, man!" Guy slaps his forehead. "I should have guessed it. This is a trap."

"Of course it's a trap, you delightful idiot." Scarlett smirks. "You're standing in a ring of proximity mines, which I have just activated. If either of you tries to leave, you'll be blown to bits."

"You're the worst party planner *ever*," you say.

"Sorry. It's not really my job. I work in corporate espionage." She turns to Guy. "As for you, what happened? I waited for you at the temple for hours!"

"I had a change of heart," Guy says stubbornly.

"Great. Some partner you turned out to be."

"Let me guess what happens next," you say. "We throw you the idol, and you deactivate the mines with that remote you've got in your hand?"

Scarlett nods. "Exactly. Once I've run a long way away, of course. Can't have you catching me, can I?"

To throw the idol to Scarlett like she wants, go to page 114.

To stand your ground and refuse to give it to her, go to page 122.

"Which way?" you ask.

"Back down into the ruins," Karma says. "It's too big to follow us there!"

You both climb down the side of the pyramid as fast as you can. The ground shakes as the demon monkey bounds closer and closer.

You hope Karma's right. Down among the ruined buildings, where trees have broken through the stone paving, there are gaps too narrow for a giant demon monkey to fit through. As you make your way there, you hear the ripping, wrenching sound of trees being torn up by the roots.

"So much for that idea," Karma gasps. "Looks like a few trees won't slow the beast down."

You spot a stone building that's still mostly intact. The walls look thick enough to resist a giant demon monkey's fists. Without stopping to think, you dash through the doorway. Karma follows.

"Did it see where we went?" you ask.

Karma puts her finger to her lips for silence. She looks out. "It's hunting for us," she whispers.

It dawns on you that there are no exits from this little stone room other than the one you came in by. You're trapped.

"Get ready to run the other way," Karma says solemnly. "I'll lead it off."

"It'll eat you!"

"Not if I'm quick. And I *am* quick. Fastest legs in the East." She winks. "See you around. Good luck!"

Before you can say another word, Karma runs from the building. You hear her yelling, and the demon monkey chasing her. You wonder if you'll ever see her again . . .

You have to keep moving. Turn to page 116.

Feeling terrible, you toss the idol out of the clearing. Scarlett laughs and scoops it up into her arms, cradling it like a baby. "It's beautiful," she purrs. "So precious . . ."

You and Guy exchange looks. "I didn't have a choice," you say miserably.

"I know," he sighs. "It's just too bad."

Scarlett climbs to the top of a nearby rock formation and presses a button on her gizmo, which starts the mines beeping. "The mines will switch off in five minutes," she says. "I'd say that's a fair head start, wouldn't you?"

"You won't get away with this!" growls Guy.

Scarlett laughs. "I already have!"

Next second, a demon monkey crashes into the area, ripping its way through the trees. It ignores both you and Guy and heads straight for Scarlett.

With a cry of fear, she takes off running. The last you see of her, she's sprinting down one of the long stone paths with the idol under her arm, the demon monkey pounding along behind her.

As soon as the mines stop beeping, you and Guy get out of there.

Eventually, after many more adventures, you make it back to civilization . . . but without the idol or Scarlett as proof, nobody believes your story.

At least you and your good friend Guy know the truth. One day, this will all make a great story for your grandkids . . .

116

You're alone, making your way through the jungle, looking for a place where you can take shelter. Night fell a long time ago. Only the feeble light of the moon keeps you from stumbling around in the pitch-darkness.

Fortunately, you've found one of the stone paths that crisscross the jungle, and this one is pretty much intact. You have to hope it leads somewhere. Shadowy shapes loom up around you. They're only statues, ugly and staring in the moonlight, but they still creep you out.

You follow the path, sidestepping white things that look like bones, until finally you reach a gaping cave mouth set into the side of a mountain. At least it'll keep the rain off if the weather turns bad. You slip inside and see, in the darkness at the back of the cave, a glimmer of golden light.

Carefully, you approach. The golden light is coming from an idol, bathed in a shaft of moonlight filtering in from a gap in the cave roof. *I must be in a temple*, you realize, peering closely at the idol.

Is that thing made of *solid gold*? It can't be. It would be worth a fortune if it was.

Farther inside, past the idol's pedestal, you see a stone-walled tunnel leading into the mountainside. There could be a whole labyrinth of paths in there. Better not go any farther in.

Do you dare to take the idol? It would make a fantastic prize for your birthday scavenger hunt, that's for sure. And such a valuable artifact deserves to be in a museum—not hidden away in a remote, crumbling temple.

The more you stare, the more really good reasons you come up with for why you ought to grab the idol.

So that's what you do.

The instant your fingers touch the smooth gold, pounding feet shake the floor. You glance up and

see a gigantic, skull-headed demon monkey running toward you. It looks really, really angry. Somehow you don't think it would help if you put the idol back.

With the idol under your arm, you run. You run the only way you can go—into the tunnels.

If you have Guy Dangerous's machete, run to page 130.

If you have Scarlett Fox's compass, run to page 125.

If you have Karma Lee's lucky talisman, run to page 141.

If you don't have any of these, go to page 121.

You skid to a halt next to Guy. He's clinging onto the ledge, while the demon monkey clings onto him. You pull out the machete and swing it, blunt side down, at the demon monkey's knuckles. *Thwack.*

The demon monkey grunts in pain and surprise. It obviously didn't expect its prey to fight back. You slam the machete down again and again until the demon monkey lets Guy go. It whines, sounding strangely sad as it huddles into the tunnel mouth, nursing its sore paw.

Guy pulls himself back up and shakes himself. "You saved my life," he says in shock. "I . . . I ought to tell you something. I've got to make this right."

"Save it for later," you say. "Let's get out of here."

★

Much later, once you're sure the demon monkey is no longer following, you make camp. On a raised stone platform dotted with statues, you and Guy build a small fire and sit around it. You're crazy tired, but too wired to sleep.

"I'm sorry, kid. I should have told you sooner. This was all a setup," Guy says in a quiet, guilty voice. "The plane crash? It wasn't an accident. We meant to come here. It was all Scarlett's idea."

"Why?" you want to know.

"She didn't tell me everything. But it's all to do with an idol. That idol you've got there, in fact. I was supposed to meet her at the temple."

"To steal it?"

"Yeah. But I couldn't go through with it. I came looking for you instead."

"I'm glad you did," you tell him. "You came through when it mattered. So thanks."

In the morning, you see a column of red smoke in the distance—a signal!

To head straight for it and get there quickly, go to page 110.

To take a longer, roundabout route and try to sneak up on the signal sender, go to page 58.

You make it five paces into a tunnel when you trip over a rock and crash to the floor. The demon monkey looms over you. It looks hungry.

Sadly, demon monkeys don't live on burgers and fries. *Chomp*.

"You'll never get this idol from me!" you yell, sounding braver than you feel. You know she's got you trapped.

But suddenly, with a huge bellow, a huge demon monkey and a horde of little ones come crashing through the trees. There are no eyes in those empty eye sockets, but if there were, they would be glaring at you in anger. They want the idol back, and they're not leaving without it.

"Run!" Scarlett screams.

"What about the mines?" you yell.

"They aren't even activated."

"WHAT?"

"I was bluffing! Do I have to spell it out?" Scarlett sprints past you and across the clearing, away from the demon monkeys. She doesn't explode.

Guy is furious. "Why, that weaselly little . . ."

"Worry about it later," you say. "We need to run!"

All three of you scramble up the rocky slope and dash along the stone path, pursued by the demon monkey and his crowd of little friends. Are they related, you wonder? You don't stop to ask.

Now that you're on the same side as Scarlett again, you work together to escape. Guy points out the safest ground to run on and Scarlett uses her zip-line to whizz you all across the gap between two ruined buildings. Eventually, you lose the demon monkeys.

Much later that day, you run into a TV news crew out hunting for you. Millions of people across the world see you hold up the idol in triumph. Scarlett looks bitter, but you know she won't try anything in front of the cameras.

You make it back home, weary but alive. The idol ends up in a museum. You never made it to your party, though, and you often find yourself wondering what else you missed out on, back in the jungle . . .

RUN AGAIN? TURN TO PAGE 9

You run and run, leaving Guy to save himself. You hear a long, drawn-out scream seconds later.

Unfortunately, because Guy isn't around anymore, he's not there to help you when you sprint right into the middle of a huge patch of quicksand.

Fortunately, you remember the way to survive falling into quicksand: don't panic, and move as little as possible. You take off your jacket and spread it out to give yourself a surface to press on.

I'm going to make it, you think.

And then you see the demon monkey at the edge of the quicksand, tossing a huge boulder and catching it. It seems almost amused.

It flings the boulder at you.

You do not make it. Sorry!

RUN AGAIN? TURN TO PAGE 9

You sprint into the temple tunnels with the demon monkey close on your heels. Fortunately, the tunnels have lots of junctions and turnings. By running one way, then the other, you manage to leave the demon monkey behind.

The bad news is that you're now lost in a maze of tunnels. Tucking the idol under one arm—it's heavy, actually—you take out Scarlett's compass and work out which way is which. Then you steadily pick your way through the tunnels and soon make it outside. Apart from a scary moment when you hear the demon monkey breathing around the corner, it's an easy run. Feeling confident, you emerge from the temple into the shadow of a ruined building whose walls are overgrown with vines.

It's pitch-black, and a rumble in the air tells you a storm is brewing. As you hunker down in the corner of a ruin to get as much shelter as you can, you overhear an angry voice muttering.

"Blast that dimwit, where is he? Come on, Guy, it's been three hours! Oh, who am I kidding? He's not coming."

It's Scarlett Fox! You sneak a look around the side of the wall. She's on her own, glancing at her watch and fiddling with one of her gadgets. Scarlett screams when you step out of the darkness.

"What's the matter?" you say. "Did you think you'd seen a ghost?" You advance. She stumbles backward. Thunder crashes overhead, and a lightning flash lights up the ruins around you.

"I'm just surprised to see you!" she stammers. "I'm sorry about any, erm, misunderstandings we . . ."

You can't resist showing her the idol. It *has* to be what she's been after this whole time. "Hoping to find this?"

Scarlett gasps. She runs at you, maddened with greed—and trips over a tree root. Her yell of pain as she falls is almost drowned out by a fresh crack of thunder. She rolls around on the ground, clutching her leg. It looks like she's badly hurt, but you hardly know whether to trust anything she does anymore.

Then a blinding flash leaves you blinking and

dazzled. Lightning forks down out of the sky, striking the roots of the very tree that Scarlett tripped over! It bursts into flame instantly.

How could lightning strike so close? You were almost burned to a cinder! Maybe this idol you're carrying is bad luck?

"Help me!" Scarlett wails, still huddled on the ground. "I can't stand up!"

The fire is spreading from tree to tree now. You hear the crackle of branches going up in flames. Soon, this whole part of the jungle will be burning.

It's decision time. You might be able to carry Scarlett out of here, but not the idol, too. You're going to have to leave one of them behind.

To rescue Scarlett and abandon the idol, turn to page 137.

To abandon Scarlett and escape with the idol, turn to page 132.

You reach your destination, the stone column standing like a signpost in the middle of the tangled jungle. There's a black SUV with tinted windows waiting there. To your horror, a pair of beefy men in camouflage gets out and grabs you!

"Get off me!" you yell. "What are you doing?"

"Shut up," grunts one of the goons.

A man in a suit rolls down the SUV window. He's wearing dark glasses. "Agent Renarde," he drawls. "Where is the idol we paid you to recover?"

"You'll have it soon," Scarlett says. "Sorry, sir."

"I do not tolerate delays, agent."

"No, sir. Sorry, sir. Won't happen again."

You wonder where her attitude has gone. Bold, glamorous Scarlett suddenly looks *meek*.

"What do we do with the kid?" says a goon.

The man in the suit glances at you. "That presents a problem. With a possibly fatal solution."

"Hang on!" Scarlett yells. "Let's use that cave over there as a holding cell while I fetch the idol."

Your hands are tied together with rope, and then

you're blindfolded and marched into somewhere echoey and cold. "Sit down, shut up, and don't move," one of the goons tells you gruffly. Then you hear boots stomping off.

The SUV engine starts and you hear it pull away.

Time passes. Water drips. Nobody returns.

As you wait miserably in the dark, wondering what to do next, you suddenly hear Guy Dangerous calling your name from outside. The guards told you to stay quiet, but do you? Could it be a test?

To call out an answer to Guy, go to page 134.

To stay silent, go to page 138.

You run through the temple corridors, turning this way and that, trying to shake off the nightmarish giant demon monkey. Any second now, he might chase you down a dead end and you'll be trapped.

At the end of one tunnel, you see moonlight shining through an opening to the outside world. You're saved, if you can make it through. The only problem is, the opening's blocked with a mass of thick, tangled vines.

You remember Guy's machete!

A few slashes, and you've cut your way through the barrier. You dive through just as the demon monkey comes around the corner behind you. It charges, bellowing.

Your moment of triumph turns to disaster as you find yourself on a stone balcony. You're outside, but there's nowhere to go. The ground is far below you.

"Hey! Grab my hand!" It's Guy's voice, coming

from above. You look up to see him hanging over a ledge, reaching out for you. You gratefully grab his hand and he swings you up to safety. The demon monkey crashes out of the opening, stumbles over the balcony, and falls, howling.

"Good timing!" you tell Guy.

He grins. "Come on, let's get out of here."

The ledge Guy pulled you up to adjoins a path down the side of the mountain. As you begin to walk down it, Guy yells in alarm. To your horror, the demon monkey has flung an arm over and grabbed Guy by the leg! It must have caught hold of the balcony on the way down and hauled itself up.

"Run!" Guy yells. "Save yourself!"

To save your own skin, run to page 124.

To dash back up the path and try to save Guy, go to page 119.

You clutch the idol tightly and run and run without looking back. The fire quickly spreads. Before long, half the mountainside is ablaze.

The smoke and the fire attract a passing plane, and before long you're rescued. You never make it to the party, but after all you've been through, you're not exactly in a party mood.

The idol is confiscated and ends up in a museum. You go back to your everyday life, but you're haunted by guilty thoughts. You don't sleep well. You try not to think about what happened to Scarlett. Then, one night, in the middle of a storm, there's a knock on your door. A hoarse-sounding British voice croaks, "Mind if I hang out?"

Uh-oh. This has gotten a bit creepy . . .

"I'm getting us out of here," you yell. "I've got a party to get to!"

Leaving the film crew behind, you fly out of the jungle over miles and miles of featureless land until you finally reach a town. From there, you're able to travel to Palomar Beach. Scarlett calls a rescue team to fetch Guy, who she feels guilty about abandoning.

Palomar Beach is every bit as awesome as the brochures made it sound. For a whole weekend, you kick back and relax with your closest friends, playing games, relaxing on the beach, and helping yourself to all the food in the fridge. You Jet Ski over the blue rolling waves. You sleep by open campfires on the warm sand.

And then, on Monday, there's a knock on the door. It's the police. They are not amused. It turns out Zack Wonder's film company didn't take kindly to the theft of company property. You're going to be grounded for a LONG time. End of the road!

"In here, Guy!" you shout.

You brace yourself, wondering if the guards will rush in. But the only sound is Guy's whoop of joy as he sees you. He pulls off your blindfold and slashes your bonds with a stout knife.

"Thanks for coming back for me," you tell him.

Guy gives you a drink of water from his hip flask. "You would've done the same for me," he says. Then he sighs. "I'm sorry that I ever got involved in Scarlett's setup. I feel terrible about it."

That confirms it, you think—the plane crash was a fake. "Where are Scarlett and the others?" you ask.

"They got away," he tells you. "I watched them hightail it out of the jungle with that idol on board. Any minute now, they'll be taking off. Scarlett's boss has a private plane just down on the coast."

As you think things over, you realize something doesn't add up. "If Scarlett's people have all this gear so close by—SUVs and planes and stuff—then how come you needed to rig our plane crash? Why didn't they just come in and fetch the idol if they wanted it so badly?"

"Because Scarlett's corporation isn't allowed to just go hunting for treasure in other people's countries," Guy explains. "A rescue operation, on the other hand? They can get away with that."

You hear the distant drone of a plane going by.

You and Guy stand outside and watch a small plane pass by overhead. *Scarlett's in there*, you think.

Guy pats your shoulder. "That idol was bad luck, kid. You're better off without it, trust me."

As you watch, lightning strikes the plane. One of the engines catches fire. The plane begins to lose altitude.

You and Guy exchange looks. "You know, Guy, I think you're right."

The last thing you see of the plane is a flaming streak vanishing into the horizon.

★

Over the next few days, you and Guy gradually work your way out of the jungle and back to civilization.

You're sunburned, bug-bitten, and hungry, but alive. You hardly even care about missing the party.

Weirdly, there's nothing in the news about Scarlett. Was the crash hushed up, or did the plane make it safely back to land? Is she in the jungle now, still clinging to the idol, running away from demon monkeys?

You'll never know—but you can't help wondering.

Even if she is a liar and a thief, you can't leave Scarlett. You put the idol down beside the path, hoping you'll be able to find it again. The heat from the burning trees is intense.

You pull Scarlett's arm over your shoulder and you hobble off together. Behind you, a tree topples over with a crash, sending glowing sparks into the sky. In the distancc you hear the demon monkey's wild howl. "Which way?" you gasp.

"Down . . . the side . . . of the hill," she gasps. "There's a broken stone column about half a mile away. Easy to see. That's where we're heading."

"Why? What's there?"

"Our ticket out of this place!"

With many looks over your shoulder to see if the demon monkey is coming, you help Scarlett away from the burning jungle and into the cool darkness at the bottom of the hill.

You spot the broken column peeping through the vine-draped trees.

Run on to page 128.

Guy calls your name several times, sounding like he's losing hope. Eventually, he gives up.

You're held captive for a long time. After what must be ten or twelve hours, you decide the guards aren't coming back. You have a blindfold on and your hands are tied, but you can still walk. You could even run!

You get to your feet and stagger toward what you hope is the exit. Luckily, you make it outside. Unluckily, there's a demon monkey waiting for you. He snatches you up as if you were an enormous banana. *Nom nom!*

"You want the idol so much, Scarlett? TAKE IT!" You shove the idol into Scarlett's hands and run like mad.

For one glorious moment, she doesn't know whether to keep it or throw it away. Then, as if someone had blown a whistle, all the demon monkeys charge in, screaming.

You can hear fighting behind you—demon monkeys squealing, Guy shouting, Scarlett shrieking, and the guards thumping and kicking. But they'll have to fend for themselves, because you're already running.

Just as you're reaching a crossroads in the jungle, you hear a shout behind you. "Hey! Wait up!"

It's Karma Lee, covered in bloody scratches, but still very much alive. "Planning on exploring this jungle on your own, were you?" she says jokingly.

"What happened back there?" you ask. "Are Guy and Scarlett . . . OK?"

"For now," Karma says, as if it didn't much matter either way. "I think they're trying to reach a helicopter somewhere nearby. Between you and me, I think the demon monkeys already trashed it."

"So, what now?" you ask.

"We keep going. I already told you we make a good team. If we watch each other's backs, we'll survive this."

That is how the adventures begin. Over the next seven weeks, you and Karma Lee beat a path through the jungle, discovering even more ruins, unopened tombs, ghastly statues, and halls full of withered mummies. You run from twisted creatures with their heads on backward, hairy things like half-men half-bats, and even the legendary chupacabra. By the time you arrive back in civilization, you have enough stories to last a lifetime. One day, you think, Hollywood will make a movie of them.

Even after all that, though, you still don't know what happened to the golden idol . . .

You rush through the corridors of the temple, with the idol heavy in your arms and the demon monkey close behind. Its inhuman screech rings in your ears. You have to get away, or that thing will have you for lunch!

Maybe Karma Lee's talisman can help. You grab it as you run, and wish, harder than you've ever wished for anything, for some good luck right now.

Oh, great. Up ahead is a rickety bridge over a pit. Looks like the opposite of good luck. With nowhere else to go, you charge across it. The demon monkey bounds after you, makes a flying leap to grab you—and smashes straight through the old bridge. You glance back and see nothing but falling timbers. The demon monkey is gone!

As if that wasn't enough good luck, the very next turn you take leads you out onto the mountainside. You're on a narrow path with a frightening drop to one side, but you're alive and you have the idol. You take a deep breath, smelling the sweet fresh air.

"Found you!" shouts Karma Lee, running up the

path toward you. “Glad to see you made it. Is that . . . the idol? I have heard so much about this treasure.”

“Sure looks like it is. I don’t think the demon monkey liked me taking it.”

Karma shrugs. “Well, too late to give it back now. Come on. We need to get out of this ruined city, and those monsters won’t stop chasing us.”

You run behind her, heading away from the ruins and back toward the jungle. You realize with a shudder that you’re not just running back to civilization—you’re running for your life!

You work your way around the side of the mountain on a narrow, crumbling rock ledge. Ahead, to the right, is a dark cave mouth. The jungle sprawls below you. Karma grabs your shoulder and points out a patch of jungle where lights are shining. You could swear they’re spotlights.

To enter the cave mouth, run to page 93.

To keep running down to the lit-up patch of jungle, run to page 102.

"Thank you. I knew you were a sensible kid." Once she has the idol, Scarlett's all sweetness and light. She's true to her word, too. Even the guards in their uniforms are polite to you, once they see you're not going to cause any more trouble.

As the sun rises over the jungle, a black helicopter comes into view. It sets down in the middle of the camp, and everyone climbs aboard.

You are dropped off at your birthday party. You see your best friends swarming toward the helicopter, waving and shouting. It's a great sight. Soon, the jungle is all but forgotten as you enjoy the company of your friends, the amazing food, the swimming, and the sunshine.

You never hear of the idol again. You can only hope its strange magic won't cause any problems in the outside world . . . You can't help but think that maybe you should have kept hold of it. Where did Karma go? And whatever happened to Guy?

You work your way slowly around the outside of the base camp, trying to be as stealthy as you can. Next moment, klaxons blare and searchlights blaze all around you. The corporate army is back from the temple early! You and Karma freeze as people come running from all sides. Suddenly, it seems this is the most populated part of the jungle.

"Stay where you are!" yells Scarlett Fox, running in from one direction. A group of corporate roughnecks in combat uniforms come with her. They all look ready to rumble. This isn't good.

Then Guy Dangerous comes running from the opposite side, with a torn rag tied around his head and a machete in his hand. "Back off, Scarlett!" he shouts. "Leave the kid alone. If you want your precious idol, you're going to have to bargain for it."

"What if I just take it by force?" says Scarlett, cocking her head.

"Then you've got to go through me," Guy says, coming to join you.

"And me," says Karma. She leaps into a fighting

stance. Suddenly, the guards don't look as ready to rumble as they did a second ago.

Scarlett sighs heavily and face-palms. "Why does everything have to be so complicated . . ."

A roar from the trees nearby tells you that things are about to get a lot more complicated.

All around, skull-headed demon monkeys begin to drop out of the tree branches. First one, then two, then ten, then *hundreds*. They creep closer and closer, surrounding you, Guy, Karma, Scarlett, and the corporate guards.

A row of dark-eyed skull faces stares at you. You'll see it in your nightmares for a long time to come—if you ever make it out of here alive. Which doesn't look very likely.

"This changes things," says Karma.

"Yup," says Guy. "Out of the frying pan . . ."

"I guess we're all on the same side now?" you tell Scarlett.

Scarlett holds her empty hands up and shouts to the demon monkeys: "I haven't got your idol, understand? I didn't steal it! It's not me you want, it's them!"

The demon monkeys don't seem to care. They just keep advancing. You're almost completely hemmed in now. Everywhere you look, you see a tide of the hideous things. There's only one gap in the circle, and it's closing fast.

"The idol is the key," Karma says to you urgently. "You must decide what to do!"

Do you throw the idol to the demon monkeys? Turn to page 149.

Do you give it to Scarlett? Turn to page 139.

Or do you keep the idol and run for your life through the gap? Turn to page 151.

You count *one, two, three* . . . and then you run, shoving Scarlett aside like an American football player.

Her disbelieving cry rings out. "You are KIDDING me!"

You run through the camp. Guards look at you, bewildered, as you run past. Scarlett chases after you, yelling at the top of her voice. "You idiot! Where do you think you're going to go?"

You don't bother to answer her. You just keep running, away from the spotlights, back into the confusing darkness of the jungle. Behind you, you hear Scarlett yelling at her goons to get after you, stop you, get that blasted idol back!

"Come on, Karma!" you gasp, still running hard. "I need you!"

The sun's starting to come up. You've slept a little and the food you've had has given you energy. Up ahead, on a ridge, is a standing figure. Karma? No—it's Guy! Nothing for it but to trust him.

"This way!" he shouts. "Down to the river!"

With the idol safe under your arm, you follow. The guards are chasing you now. You hear one of them gasp as he runs into a low-hanging branch. Trees hurt! Another guard, faster than the others, is gaining on you. You could go faster if you drop the idol . . . but you just can't bring yourself to do it.

Then there's a familiar shout, a sharp crack, and the guard goes tumbling to the ground, unconscious. Karma Lee runs up alongside you. "Better late than never!" she puffs.

Guy leads you both down to the river, where he's hidden a stolen motor dinghy. The engine starts on the first try. Together, you all make it out of the jungle, leaving Scarlett empty-handed and furious on the riverbank.

You did it! But how did Scarlett's story end, you wonder? You'll have to run again if you want to find out.

"OK. Let's hope this works."

You swing your arms back, then fling the idol as hard as you can. The demon monkeys swarm around it and hoist it on to their furry little shoulders like football players celebrating a touchdown. They make an excited squeaking, hissing noise.

"Run!" Guy yells. "They're distracted!"

You make a break for it. Scarlett, Guy, and Karma lead the way, followed by you, with the corporate goons bringing up the rear. Some of them trip and fall, and some tumble into pits, but you don't have time to see if they make it. You have to get out of this jungle alive.

Eventually, you reach a clearing where a black helicopter is parked. Scarlett fires it up, grumbling under her breath about that "stupid idol" and how her boss is going to kill her for coming back empty-handed.

"Not so fast," Guy tells her. "Your meeting with your boss can wait. You have a party to take us to first, remember?"

Scarlett stares. "You can't be serious. That was just part of the cover story!"

"Fine. Move over and let me drive."

And drive he does. Well, *fly*. Guy insists on flying you all the way to Palomar Beach, so you'll arrive in plenty of time for your party.

Thinking it over, you've done pretty well. You may be leaving the jungle without the idol, but your party has an extra guest in the form of Karma Lee. She gets involved with everything, from smashing the piñata to pieces with a single kick to taking you on an awesome treasure hunt—and luckily, this one has no demon monkeys.

With the idol under your arm, you run. And you never, ever stop.

You run through the jungle, weaving in and out of the trees. You reach a stone path, jump up on to it, and run along that. When the path branches, you choose a direction and swerve off, running down a new path.

You leap over traps, duck out of the way of whizzing blades, and skid under stone barriers. Sometimes you swing over broken sections, sometimes you jump. Soon, you forget how long it's been since you ate or drank.

The sun sets. You keep running. The sun rises. You keep running. The next day, the same thing happens. Where is this energy coming from? Perhaps the idol's magic is keeping you going. You know one thing for sure—if you stop, or slow down, then *it* will get you. You're not sure if it's one big demon monkey or lots of little ones, but it picked up your trail a long time ago, and it will not stop chasing you.

You have no way to keep track of time. Eventually, it all merges into one. You have the idol, and you run. That's all that matters.

Sometimes, on the long, lonely stretches of stone path, you think you remember someone you used to be. Something about a party? People called Guy and Scarlett? A plane crash . . . then, just as quickly, you forget again.

Turn to page 151.

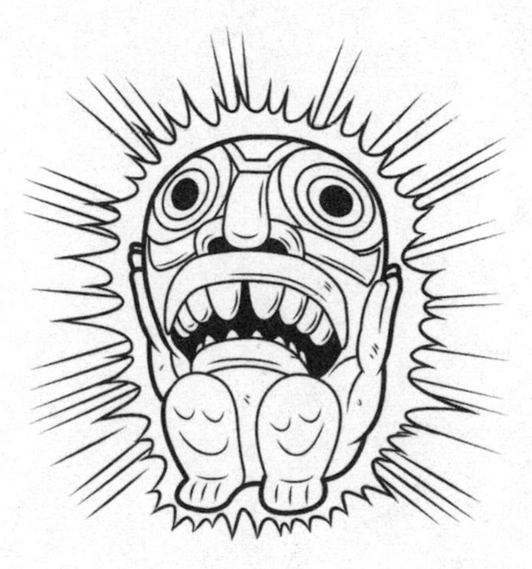